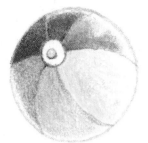

SHARE YOUR RAINBOW

18 ARTISTS DRAW THEIR HOPE FOR THE FUTURE

INTRODUCTION BY R. J. PALACIO

Random House 🏠 New York

 BRIAN BIGGS

 CORINNA LUYKEN

 DAN SANTAT
COVER ARTIST

 CÁTIA CHIEN

 MAGDALENA MORA

 LAURA VACCARO SEEGER

 VASHTI HARRISON

 OGE MORA

 BOB SHEA

 MOLLY IDLE

 ELISE PARSLEY

 LANE SMITH

 SARAH JACOBY

 JEROME PUMPHREY & JARRETT PUMPHREY

 DIVYA SRINIVASAN

 CLAIRE KEANE

 ADAM REX

 SHANNON WRIGHT

 ISABEL ROXAS

IN GREEK MYTHOLOGY, the rainbow was personified as a young goddess named Iris. She was usually depicted as having wings, and because she was swift as the wind, she was also a messenger of the gods. She was a literal bridge between the heavens and the earth, traveling from one world to the other, leaving in her wake a vapor trail of colors that arched across the sky. That rainbow of colors was a symbol of hope, even back then, at the very dawn of civilization. And it remains one for people now all over the world.

Human beings have always recognized in rainbows a kind of magic. A rainbow is just so beautiful, so fleeting, that to see one is to feel like you've actually caught a glimpse of true almighty wonder, like a wink from the universe. Whether it's a rainbow in the sky, or in the glimmer of a puddle, or in the drawings by children being put in windows and drawn on sidewalks in uncertain times, rainbows are messages of love and hope and peace.

I am astounded by rainbows. I am humbled by them. I am delighted by them. I am in awe of them. I feel peace because of them. And I will continue to look for them as I walk through this world, in the sky and in the puddles and in the windows and on the sidewalks, as a gentle reminder that they are always nearby, somewhere beyond our grasp and yet never really beyond our reach.

—R. J. Palacio

I cannot wait to yak with my neighbors,
and laugh with my neighbors,
and snarf up toasted marshmallows
with my neighbors.

New places await,

where I'll be welcomed
by smiling faces

and share food with friends.

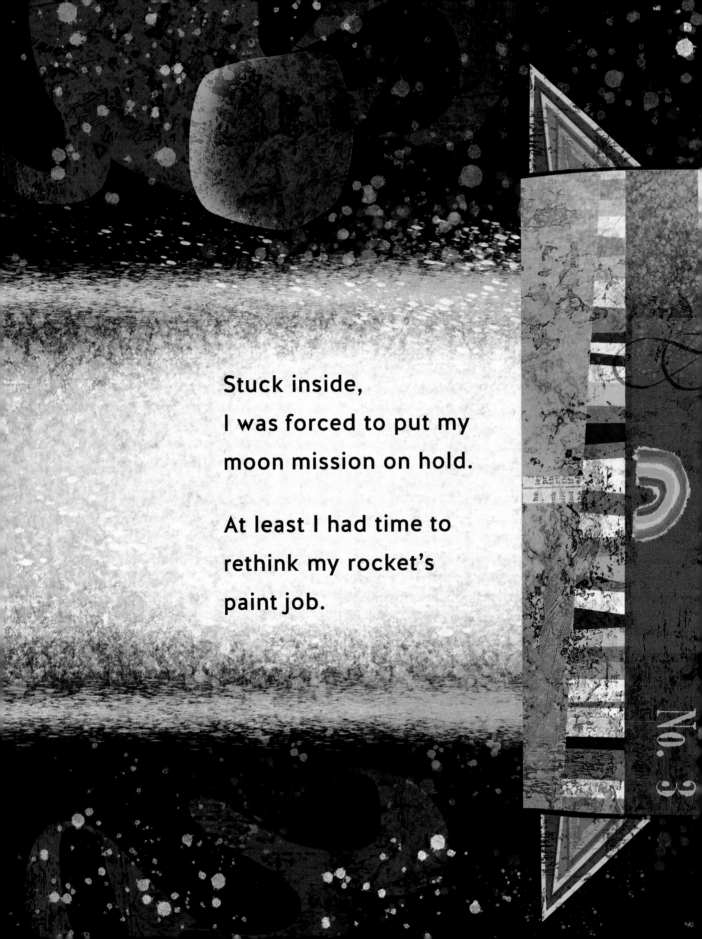

Stuck inside,
I was forced to put my
moon mission on hold.

At least I had time to
rethink my rocket's
paint job.

No. 3

I can't wait to *ride* a rainbow.

I hope I can go to the park
with my best friend and
pet all the dogs.

BARK
BARK

And enjoy ice cream at the beach—with friends.

My rainbow is playing
ball with everyone.

Mine is sitting next to strangers on the bus.

Mine is the sweet treat
of a happy birthday!

We will go swimming
and play in the water.

And hit up the roller rink
with my friends to skate
the night away.

My rainbow shows
crowded laps,

loud dinners,

and cozy cousin bedtimes.

I'm looking forward to being kinder to our Earth.

And to seeing the world
through a new lens, imagining
a universe of possibilities.

We will hold hands
as we walk
and talk
and listen
and be . . .

together.

Soon, with sun, my garden will have
a rainbow growing, a rainbow to harvest,
and a rainbow to share with family and friends.

My rainbow is a warm hug.

What's your rainbow?

Share yours on social media by
tagging @RandomHouseKids
and use #sharemyrainbow

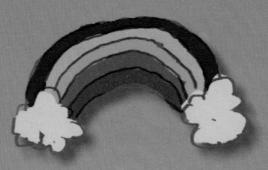

Copyright © 2020 by Penguin Random House LLC
All rights reserved. Published in the United States by Random House Children's Books,
a division of Penguin Random House LLC, New York.
Random House and the colophon are registered trademarks of Penguin Random House LLC.

Visit us on the Web!
rhcbooks.com
Educators and librarians, for a variety of teaching tools,
visit us at RHTeachersLibrarians.com

Library of Congress Cataloging-in-Publication Data is available upon request.
ISBN 978-0-593-37521-1 (trade pbk.) – ISBN 978-0-593-37397-2 (ebook)

The text of this book is set in 18-point GR Halis.
Interior design by Rachael Cole

Printed in the United States of America
10 9 8 7 6 5 4 3 2 1

First Edition